Mitch and Annie

high school adventures

by
Jane Christensen

Watermill Press

Printed in the United States of America

Illustrations by Thomas Heggie

ISBN 0-89375-747-0

Contents

My Brother, the Matchmaker

Sometimes I wish I didn't have a brother. My brother Mitch always gets to do things I can't do because he's older. He's also bigger, noisier, and messier. And he says things like, "What did you do to your hair, Annie? Are you trying out for clown school?"

On the other hand, Mitch is a friend of Craig Taylor's. I think Craig is just about perfect. If Mitch helps me meet Craig, I will forgive Mitch for everything he's ever done to me.

It's funny, though. Craig comes over to our house a lot, but he's never been here when I'm home. That's driving me crazy. So I decided that Monday, I would be home when Mitch and Craig got back from track practice. I came straight home from school to be sure to get here first.

I heard Mitch call as he came in. "Hi, Mom, I'm home. Craig's here."

"Hi, Mitch. Hi, Craig," Mom called from the back of the house. "There's juice in the refrigerator."

"Thanks, Mom," Mitch said.

"Thanks, Mrs. Parker," Craig called.

6

He was really here. I could just walk into the kitchen and say "hi" to him. I felt my heart pounding. I was scared. *All right, Annie,* I told myself. *Now's your chance.*

I pushed the kitchen door open.

"Hi, Mitch. Oh, hi," I said to Craig.

"Annie, what are you doing home so early?" Mitch asked.

"I had to study for a test, so I came straight home." I gave Craig my sweetest smile. He smiled back.

"Hi," Craig said to me, in a low voice. He talked as if we shared a secret together. I blinked to keep from staring.

Then Mitch spoke up. "Hey, listen, Craig. I have to take the car downtown. Do you want a ride home?"

"That's okay, I can walk," said Craig.

"No, be my guest. Save your body for the track meet." Mitch almost dragged

Annie pushed the kitchen door open.

him out of the room.

"Mitch!" I grabbed him. "What's going on?"

"I almost forgot, Annie. I told Dad I'd meet him downtown with the car. See you later."

Mitch ran out, pulling Craig along with him.

What happened? Everything was fine until Mitch messed it up.

After dinner, I waited until Mom and Dad settled down in the living room. Then I said to Mitch, "Come out on the porch with me. I have to talk to you."

Mitch and I sat on the swing. We talked low so no one could hear us.

"Mitch, what was going on with Craig this afternoon? Why did you rush him out of here?"

"Oh, I was just kidding around with him."

I decided to tell Mitch the real reason I wanted to know. Then maybe he would tell me the truth.

"Um, don't say anything to Craig about this, but I kind of like him," I stammered.

Mitch was quiet.

"Mitch?" I asked.

"Annie, I don't know how to say this. I like Craig. But I don't want you to like him. And don't ever tell anyone I said so."

"Why not? What's wrong with him?" I asked.

"He dates a lot of girls. He always talks about how much they like him. He doesn't seem to care about any of them. He even said to me once, 'All I have to do is tell a girl she has beautiful eyes. Then she falls for me.' He thinks he's a real ladies' man."

"Don't say anything to Craig about this, but I kind of like him," Annie stammered.

"Thanks for telling me." Now I knew why Mitch acted funny this afternoon. "You didn't want me to talk to him today, did you?"

"Yeah, that's right," he muttered.

"Okay," I said. "But I still want to meet him."

"Well, don't look at me. I'm not going to help you."

"Wait a minute," I was getting mad. "I'm not a kid."

"But he hurts people, Annie."

Maybe Craig wasn't as nice as he looked. But I didn't want Mitch to think I'd fall on my face without his help. "Mitch, you told me what I need to know. Now let me worry about it. Are you saying I can't take care of myself?"

"I don't know. If you heard him talk about the girls he goes out with . . . I don't want him talking that way about you." Mitch got up. "I'll think about it."

"Come on, Mitch," I pleaded.

"I said, I'll think about it, Annie. That's the best I can do."

My best friend, Lisa, phoned the next day. She wanted to know if I finally got to meet Craig.

"No, Mitch won't help me," I told her.

"Why not?" she wondered.

"He's just being a brother." Lisa has two brothers.

"Oh. I know what you mean," she said.

Then I heard a horn blast in front of our house. I looked out the window. It was Mitch — and Craig!

"I've got to go, Lisa. Tell you why later."

"Sure. I'll talk to you later," said Lisa as she hung up.

I ran to the door to let them in.

"Hi, Mitch." Then I turned to Craig

"I've seen you around, too," said Craig.

and smiled. "Hi."

"Annie, have you met Craig Taylor?" asked Mitch.

"Hi, Craig. I've seen you around." I smiled again.

"Hi, Annie. I didn't know you were Mitch's sister until yesterday. I've seen you around, too," said Craig.

Mitch faded into the kitchen.

Craig was looking straight at me. He smiled his wonderful smile. He leaned toward me as if he were about to tell me a secret. Then he said, "Hey, Annie, did anyone ever tell you that you have beautiful brown eyes?"

"No," I said. "But somehow, I thought you might."

Go Fly a Kite

It was a bright spring Saturday. The wind just stirred the trees and snapped the wash on the clothesline. It was perfect kite weather. I grabbed the kite I had made for my science project and took it outside.

The kite was a beauty. It was a big box kite, and it was much stronger than the kind that stores sell. I had made it of wood and cloth, not paper. The kite was black and yellow.

I drove up near the lake where there was a big field. I could fly the kite without worrying about phone lines or trees. In a few minutes, I had it up in the air.

"I like that kite," said a small voice.

I looked around, and then down. A boy, maybe ten years old, was talking to me. "I like that kite," he said again.

He stood next to me. His eyes moved as he watched the kite. He didn't say anything else.

He was quiet for a long time. I let him take turns flying the kite. Then a man called to him, "Hey, Rick! Let's go."

The boy called back, "Dad, come over here and see this kite."

"That's some kite you have," the man said to Mitch.

His father walked over.

"That's some kite you have," he said to me. "I've never seen one like it. Where did you get it?"

"I made it for school."

"You made it!" He seemed surprised. I felt good that he liked the kite so much. Then he spoke to me quietly, so Rick couldn't hear. "Would you sell that kite?" he asked. "I'd like to give it to my son. He'll be ten in two weeks."

Sell the kite? Right away, I knew I didn't want to do that.

"No," I told him. "I don't want to sell it."

I looked at Rick. I wanted him to have a kite, too. He liked mine so much. "I'll tell you what," I said to his dad. "I could make one like it. It would take me a day or so. I could have it by next week—that is, if you want to wait."

19

"Let me take a closer look."

I pulled the kite in. Rick and his father both looked at it. It was well made. The wood frame was glued, and tied with string.

Rick kept looking at the kite. His father and I spoke quietly, so Rick wouldn't hear us.

"It's very good work. I'll give you eight dollars to make a kite like that for Rick."

"It's a deal," I agreed.

I gave him my name and phone number. He said he'd come get the kite the next week. He wanted Rick's kite to be red and blue, which was okay with me. I didn't know it, but I had started something.

In the next month, I made ten kites. Other people saw the kites and phoned me. Some people talked to me at the

Rick kept looking at the kite.

lake. Or, they talked to people who bought kites from me.

While driving to the lake, I would sometimes see one of my kites hanging in the air. I felt good about that.

It was like a dream.

Well, I found out dreams don't last. Things change.

The man who ran the snack shop up at the lake started selling kites. They were a lot cheaper than mine. They were just paper and thin strips of wood. But a lot of people don't want a good kite. They bought kites from him. Not many people wanted my kites anymore.

I didn't mind *that* much. *Easy come, easy go,* I said to myself. But Craig and Louis and Ron, my best friends, were really upset. I didn't know how upset they were until after I heard what they did. They did something stupid.

Craig, Ron, and Louis went up to the lake. They walked into the snack shop and bought some soda. Then they asked the man about his kites.

"Since when did you sell kites?" asked Craig.

"People here fly them, so I sell them," replied the man.

"Oh yeah?" said Ron. "We have a friend who sells kites too."

"He used to sell a lot," added Louis. "Now he doesn't sell so many anymore."

"He was doing pretty well," said Craig, "until you started selling kites."

The three of them look pretty big when they stand close to you. The man in the shop looked worried. My friends could tell he didn't know what to do. So they thought they could make some trouble and get away with it.

Louis said, "I think I'll buy a kite." He

took out one kite after another. He looked at each one. Then Ron or Craig would say, "No, I don't like this one."

"Not as nice as Mitch's," they would say about the next kite. "Let's see another one."

The store owner tried to stop them, but they took out every kite in the shop. They spread them out on the floor of the store. No one could come in. They mixed them all up. When all the kites had been opened, Louis said, "Well, I guess he doesn't have anything I want."

"I don't see anything, either," said Craig.

"No, nothing as good as Mitch's," said Ron. "Thanks anyway." And they all walked out. The store owner just looked at the mess they had left.

The store owner knew my father. He called Dad right away.

The next day, I had to go to the lake with Ron and Louis and Craig. We spent the morning putting the kites back into their boxes. My dad said if I didn't, I couldn't use the car for a month. The same thing had happened to my friends. It's funny how parents all think alike sometimes.

I started talking to the man at the store. His name was Tony — Tony Capra. He wasn't a bad guy. When we were done, he shook hands with us. He even gave us each a free hot dog. Then he said, "I'd like to see one of these kites of yours."

I went outside. Sure enough, someone was there who had one of my kites. It was Rick, the boy who started it all. He brought his kite into the shop for Mr. Capra to look at.

"This is fine work," Mr. Capra said.

*"Okay, Mitch, it's a deal. You make them,
I sell them."*

"Listen, Mitch, I'll make you a deal. You bring a few of your kites in here, and I'll see if I can sell them."

"Mr. Capra, they sell themselves," I said. "I've got an item here no one wants to be without." I was talking just like one of the ads we both saw on our local TV station.

Mr. Capra laughed. "Okay, Mitch, it's a deal. You make them, I sell them."

"And if you run out of buyers, I'll send in these crazy guys." I looked over at my friends.

"Thanks, but no thanks," said Mr. Capra. "They might be good friends, but they are the worst customers I ever had. They just can't make up their minds."

Just Learning

Sixteen is a special birthday. Some girls want a big party. But when I'm sixteen, I want to get my driver's license. I can hardly wait.

Where I live, you have to drive to go places. I'm sick of having my mom drive me to the movies. I'm also sick of hitching rides from my friends.

My dad was going to teach me to drive. He thinks he's an ace driver. I think it's funny, the way my dad is so proud of his driving. I wanted to learn from him. But it didn't seem to be working out. One of us was always busy when the other one was free. My birthday was getting closer and closer.

When it was only a month away, I got worried. What if I needed more than one or two lessons? Would there be enough time?

My brother Mitch said, "Annie, just take a few lessons with your friends. Dad doesn't need to know. You can still go driving with him."

"Yeah, I think you're right." Mitch had a good idea for once. And I had one too. "Mitch, how about if you give me a lesson? Would you?"

There was a long silence.

"Come on, Mitch. Please?" I kept asking. Finally, he said he'd give me one lesson.

The next Sunday, he took me to the shopping center. The parking lot was almost empty. I started the car. Then I drove around the lot. And around, and around, and around. . . .

"Mitch, this is pretty dull."

"Yeah, you're right," he agreed. "I think you could drive the car part of the way home."

I started to pull out of the lot.

"Annie! Wait! A car's coming," yelled Mitch. He scared me. I stepped on the brake as hard as I could. The car stopped with a jerk. Mitch fell forward and bumped his head on the windshield.

"You can brake a *little* slower," Mitch said, rubbing his head. He looked for cars. "Okay. Now go."

I stepped on the gas. Nothing happened. Then I pressed the pedal harder. The car jumped forward. Mitch yelled, "Easy, Annie, easy!"

"I'm just learning, you know," I yelled back. Taking lessons from Mitch was a real pain. He yelled a lot.

There was so much to think about at once. Look out in front. Slow down for stop signs. Look out for kids and dogs. Look in the mirror for cars in back of you. Keep the speed steady. My head was spinning.

I was glad when that lesson was over. Mitch took the wheel and drove us home. By then, he had stopped talking to me.

It wouldn't hurt, I thought, *to have just one more lesson before I go with Dad.*

My friend Lisa's older sister, Pam,

*Annie ran the back of Pam's car up onto
a low brick wall.*

said she'd help me. She took me to the shopping center too. I was trying to back up. Somehow, I ran the back of her car up onto a low brick wall.

"How did you do that?" Pam kept asking me. "How did you do that?"

"How should I know?" I said. "I'm just learning."

Pam's boyfriend, Marty, came by at last, and helped us push the car off. But I didn't think Pam would want to give me another lesson. And I still had a few things to learn.

So I asked good old Mom.

"Of course, I won't tell Dad," she said. "He can think he's giving you your first lesson. Your first real lesson will be our secret."

"Thanks, Mom." I didn't think I needed to tell her about my *other* first lessons.

Dad said to Annie, "We've got to start those lessons."

I drove better with Mom. I drove pretty well, in fact. I just forgot to take off the hand brake. It was too bad she got so upset about that.

"How was I to know the brake was on?" I asked her. "If it doesn't stop the car, what good is it?"

But Mom didn't see it my way.

Mitch's friend, Craig, told me he'd teach me to drive on back roads. I should have known that was a line. When I drove with him, I could only use one hand. I needed the other hand to keep Craig's arm back where it belonged.

When I got back from the lesson with Craig, I didn't know anyone else to ask. But that same night at dinner, Dad said to me, "Well, Annie, your birthday is coming up. We've got to start those lessons. I'll take you Sunday for sure."

Mitch groaned. I kicked him under the table.

Sunday, Dad and I were at the parking lot. By then, I could drive there with my eyes closed.

"You're doing fine," Dad said.

"Can I take it out of the parking lot now?" I asked.

"Sure, give it a try." I pulled out of the lot. I drove home like a pro. Then I pulled into the driveway and stopped the car smoothly.

Mom and Mitch were working in the garden. They looked at Dad, waiting for the bad news.

"Mitch, your sister is some driver!" Dad said. "She learned everything just like that. She is some driver!" He went into the house.

As soon as Dad shut the door, Mitch said to me, "Some driver! Annie, you are

36

Mitch tried to squirt Annie with the hose, but she was too fast for him.

so lucky!" He tried to squirt me with the hose, but I was too fast for him.

From then on, driving was easy. I never again had to tell anyone I was "just learning."

Saturday With Cynthia

I was bored, even though it was Saturday. Nothing was happening. It was a little too hot, a little too quiet. I decided to go visit my girlfriend, Cynthia.

She lives about eight blocks away. I walked over to her house. People were sitting outside, drinking iced tea. I felt restless—everything was so quiet.

When I got to her house, she was in the driveway. She looked great, in a pair of shorts, washing the car. Her hair was so wet it looked black. She was talking to someone on the other side of the car. I sneaked up on her.

"Mitch! You scared me. Don't ever do that again!" she shrieked.

I had to laugh at her. "Do you want to come over and wash my car next?" It wasn't the first time anyone made that joke, but she laughed anyway.

"It's nice to see you," Cynthia said as she smiled at me. I felt better about the day already.

Cynthia's friend, Sandra, walked around to the front of the car. Her shoes were wet and they squished as she walked.

"Hi, Mitch," she said.

"Hi, Sandy. How is everything?"

Cynthia was in the driveway, washing the car.

"Pretty wet right now. But if we wash the car, we can use it this afternoon."

"Yeah? Where are you ladies going?" I asked.

"Downtown, to look for clothes," Sandy explained.

I made a face. "Listen, why not take the car and go up to the lake for the afternoon. Come on," I said with a grin. "Improve your tan. Make a young man happy."

"Gee, Mitch, I don't know..." Cynthia began.

"It's okay with me if you want to do something with Mitch," Sandy said. "I can go shopping by myself."

"No, you come too," I said. "Let's all go to the lake." I wanted to go with Cynthia, but Sandy was her friend, and I liked her too.

"Mitch, we really wanted to go shopping today," Cynthia said.

"Come on, honey, let's have some fun while we're young."

"I guess it would be okay," Cynthia said finally. "If we get back early enough, Sandy and I can still go shopping."

"I'll help you wash the car," I offered. "We can get some food on the way."

It was great out at the lake. We drank soda and lay in the sun. When it got too hot, we swam for a while. Cynthia's hair stayed wet and black. I liked putting my hand at the back of her neck to feel how smooth her wet hair was. When I kissed her, her face was cold from the water.

We got back just in time for dinner. I call that a fine way to spend a Saturday.

After dinner, Cynthia called. "Mitch, I want to talk to you." She sounded

Cynthia's hair stayed wet and black.

very serious.

"Sure, go ahead," I said.

"You know, I had plans for today," she began. "I wanted to go shopping with Sandy, but I didn't get to do that."

"You mean you'd rather do that than go to the lake with me?" I couldn't believe it. I like to be with her. Why didn't she want to be with me?

"Today, I wanted to go shopping. I don't want to spend all my time with you."

"Well then, go shopping as much as you want. I thought you liked me."

"I do like you. Do you like me so much that you want to do *everything* with me? You didn't want to go shopping with me."

"I don't want to be with a girl who thinks going to the lake with me is no fun."

45

"Listen to me instead of talking, will you?" She sounded mad now. What was *she* mad about? *I* was the one who was angry.

"I've heard all I want to hear," I said in an angry tone.

Cynthia didn't say anything.

"Cynthia? Are you still there?"

"I never thought you would be so un-reasonable," she said at last. "Maybe I don't like you so much after all." Then she hung up. But I didn't care. If I have to say I'm sorry for asking her to spend the day with me, who needs her?

My sister Annie walked into the room. "What happened? Is everything okay with Cynthia?"

"I don't want to talk about it," I muttered.

"Okay." Annie shrugged.

"Just a minute, Annie. If you went

46

*"What happened? Is everything okay
with Cynthia?"*

with a guy to the lake, wouldn't that be more fun than going shopping?"

"Maybe. Did you ask me that to learn about life, or is that what the fight's about?" asked Annie.

"That's the fight. She should like being with *me*, right?" I asked.

"Not all the time. Don't you like to spend time with *your* friends? Why do you spend time shooting baskets at the school yard with Louis or Ron? Why don't you ask her over to watch a game on TV?"

When my sister is right, I don't say anything. I'd feel dumb saying "Annie, you're right." She kept talking.

"You know she likes you, Mitch. You did something she didn't like, and she told you. That's no big deal."

I wasn't listening. I was thinking of Cynthia's wet black hair, and her cool face, and her smile.

"Thanks, Annie. I guess I'll call her and tell her I'm sorry I got so upset. Of course, it wasn't all *my* fault."

"Of course not, Mitch. It's never all *your* fault. I ought to know." Annie gave me a smart look.

Sisters never can quit when they're ahead.

He Loves Me, He Loves Me Not

Mike Garcia was in my English class. Whenever he raised his hand, he said something funny—not loud and funny, but quiet and funny. The more I saw him, the more I liked him. I decided to ask him to the "Ladies' Choice" dance.

It wasn't easy. Every time I'd see him, my mouth would get dry. I'd be scared my voice would sound funny. By the time I would be ready to ask him, he'd be gone.

Then, a week before the dance, I went to the store, and Mike was there. I started talking before I could think about it. I even made a joke. "Mike, what are you doing here? I thought you studied all the time."

Mike grinned at me. "I know the stuff cold. Teachers fight to give me A's."

"Uh, Mike, I wanted to ask you . . . I mean, would you go to the dance with me?"

"Sure. I'd like to," he said, smiling.

"Well, thanks. Good." I stood there like a fool. At last I said, "I guess I have some shopping to do."

"Me, too. See you in school."

*"Mike, would you like to go to the dance
with me?"*

The very next day, I overheard Susy Becker ask Mike to the dance. I knew how she'd feel when he told her "no." I felt sorry for her, and quickly walked away from them. Now I was even happier that I had asked Mike first.

I had such a good time with him at the dance! We danced every dance but one. Mike said to me, "Do you mind if I have one dance with Susy? She invited me to the dance, too. I thought I'd ask her for the next one."

"No, that's really sweet. Most guys wouldn't think of it. Go right ahead." He *was* a nice guy.

Mike walked me home. After we said good night, he leaned over and kissed me on the cheek. I danced up to my room, full of dreams.

Now it was his turn to ask me out. I was sure he would.

He walked me home after school four or five times. But each time, just when I thought he was going to ask for a date, he'd say, "See you in school." It didn't make sense. Two weeks crawled by.

Just when I couldn't stand it any longer, Mike called. At last! We made a date for the next Friday.

The day after he called me, I saw Mike at school—walking with Susy Becker. They were just talking. But I didn't like it at all.

I thought about him all day. Half the time, I didn't hear what the teachers were saying. Once, I didn't even hear the bell ring. I was busy thinking, *does Mike like me or doesn't he?* I really wanted him to. There were signs he did, and signs he didn't. *Was I doing something wrong?*

Don't worry so much, I said to myself.

54

He asked you out, didn't he?

Our date was a lot of fun. We went dancing, then we had a pizza. But when Mike took me home, he kissed me on the cheek again. I was hoping for a real kiss this time. I looked up at him.

"Mike, I don't want to put you on the spot, but how do you really feel about me? Are we friends, or what?"

Even under our porch light, I could see him turn red. I was almost sorry I'd asked. Then I heard his answer. "Annie, I think you're great!" he said. "You're fun to be with, easy to talk to, pretty..."

That was all I needed to hear. I cut right in before he could finish. "I'm sorry. I didn't mean to make you feel funny. But I'm glad I asked." I kissed him on the cheek, and ran inside.

On Monday, I looked for Mike after

"Mike, how do you really feel about me?"

school. I saw him leave the building. But Susy was with him. He was holding the door for her, and he had his other arm around her waist. When I saw them together like that, it hurt. Now I knew how he really felt.

The next day, after school, I saw Mike again. He was alone. I tried to act as if I didn't care much, but I couldn't pretend very well.

"I saw you with Susy yesterday. What's going on?" I asked.

"What do you mean?" He knew what I meant. I could tell.

"You know. You just told me how great I am. Then I saw you with your arm around her."

"I do think you're great. I'm glad we're friends," he said softly.

"Susy's great too, huh?"

"Okay, I like her a lot." I wished he

57

hadn't said that. I didn't feel calm anymore. "But I still want to be your friend," he added.

"My friend!" When I'm upset, I say what's on my mind. I can't keep it to myself. "Why did you say those things to me? You made me think I was more than a friend."

"I was trying to be nice," Mike told me. "I didn't want to hurt you."

"Nice! I was going to find out anyway. If you were nice, how come I feel this way?" Now I felt more angry than hurt. When Mike reached for my hand, I pulled away.

I walked home alone. When I got to my house, I shut myself in the bathroom and splashed cold water on my face. Then I started to hear the things that Mike had said to me. He was right too, I guess.

Annie dried her face and looked in the mirror.

He *did* like me, just not as much as I wanted him to. I hadn't thought about that. I hadn't been thinking at all. I had just been wishing. I had only seen what I wanted to see.

I dried my face and looked in the mirror. I looked okay. "Well, Annie," I said, "so this guy Mike is not for you. It's his loss, right?" The face in the mirror smiled back, just a little.

Helping a
Friend

I brought forty dollars to school with me today. I was a little nervous about it. You know, you hear stories from kids who have their bikes stolen, or their money taken. I walked to school with no trouble though. When I sat down in class, I forgot that I'd been worried.

I brought the money so I could pay for my track jacket. Well, the jackets weren't ready. I'd have to wait until next week to get mine. When I asked the coach about my money, he said I should have brought a check. He was right. Now I was stuck with forty dollars in my pocket.

I walked home late, after track practice. It was already getting dark. I still had homework to do before dinner, and I was thinking about that. Suddenly, a big guy was walking beside me. I mean, he was really big.

"Hey," he said. "Could I ask you something?"

"Go ahead," I said.

"Could you tell me where Millard Fillmore High is?" he asked.

"Yeah, sure, back that way," I said, pointing.

Mitch walked home late, after track practice.

He kept walking along with me. So I asked, "You don't live around here?"

"No, I'm visiting friends," he answered.

I looked around. No one was nearby. About three blocks ahead of us, two men walked home from work. A woman walked alone, carrying a shopping bag. I felt a little nervous because of the money. The big guy stayed with me.

"If you're looking for Millard Fillmore High, it's back that way," I said again.

"Right. I heard you say that," said the big guy.

I wondered what he was thinking. I'm in track, so I can run fast. But I'm not that big. Besides, I was carrying too much stuff to run. And I wasn't sure yet that I needed to run. He was just walking along next to me.

Finally, he asked me, "Do you live

around here?"

"No," I lied. "I'm just visiting friends."

"You know, I was wondering. Could you loan me some money?" he asked. "You see, I need it. Yes, I need it. Do you have any money with you?"

"Who, me?" I don't know why I said that. No one else was around. I guess I said it because I needed time to think about the forty dollars in my back pocket. "No, no, I don't have any money."

I was thinking as fast as I could. I didn't like this guy. I told him where the school was, and he didn't seem to care. I was so nervous, I couldn't think. But I wasn't going to give him that forty dollars. I knew that for a fact.

"Listen, buddy. What's your name?" Mr. Big asked.

"Andy. My name is Andy." I lied

"Listen, take this," Mitch said. "It's all I have."

again. Would he believe me?

"Well, Andy, now that we know each other, why don't you step around this corner with me?" This was it. Now I was worried. He was pretty close, too close. If I made a move he could grab me. And I had my gym bag and my social studies books. Why did I have to get held up the day before an exam? And where was everybody? The street was deserted.

"Uh, no thanks," I stammered. "I have to get back to my friends!"

"Oh, let's have a little talk first. I have a good reason why you should loan me some money."

"I said I don't have any money."

"Don't you want to hear my reason?" He was edging toward me. I was backing away, off the main street. I really didn't want to hear his reason.

"Uh, well, maybe I can come up with a

little cash for you. Yeah, I've got something here," I said.

I dug down into my front pockets. I pulled out about a dollar in change. I tried to sound as scared as I could. That was pretty easy to do.

"Yeah, listen. Here, take this," I said. "It's all I have." I gave him the handful of change. I know I looked as scared as I have ever looked. His big fist closed around the money.

"Now don't you feel better, helping out a friend?" He flashed me a grim smile. Then he turned up the block and started running back toward the high school.

I turned around and walked back onto the main street. Now there were people across the street, so I walked over to where they were. I noticed I had been sweating, and my heart was pounding. I

Mitch's heart was pounding.

felt shaky for a second. But that forty dollars was still in my back pocket.

I didn't feel like a hero. I had been scared. But I had kept the forty dollars. I had outsmarted the big guy. The longer I thought about it, the better I felt. When I got home, I was feeling proud of myself. I had done all right.

May the Best Person Win

Roger Martin watched me as I hung up some posters for the school play. He came over and said, "Did you make those?"

"Yes, I did," I said.

"Nice work—you're Annie Parker, aren't you?" he asked.

"Did you make those posters?"
Roger Martin asked.

"That's right."

"I'm Roger Martin." Of course I knew who he was. Everyone in school did. "I'm going to run for student body president. Maybe you could make some posters for me."

"Me?" I asked. Roger Martin wanted *my* help? Wow!

"Some people, who are working with me, are coming over to my house Saturday morning. Do you think you can come?"

"Sure!" I said. "Sure."

When I got home, the first thing I did was to tell my brother Mitch. "Guess what?" I asked. "I'm helping Roger Martin run for student body president!"

"When did you start hanging out with him?" Mitch wondered.

"He asked me today. I'm going to his house Saturday."

"Well—you're moving among the jet set of Millard Fillmore High, aren't you?" Mitch smiled at me. He knew how pleased I was.

On Saturday, I got ready for the meeting as if it were a "first date."

As I walked to Roger's house, I wondered who else would be there. I was sure to see Danny Rowan, the football star, and Karen Perkins, one of the most popular girls in the school. Maybe Anita Souza, the cheerleader, or Rod Myers, from the student council, would be there. These were the top kids in my school. I wanted to be in their group. The "Who's Who" of our high school—and me.

After I got there, Danny and Karen came in. Then Roger said, "We're all here now. You're the people who will see that I win or lose. We have a hard job. Two other good people are running—Anita Souza and Rod Myers." *So that's why they aren't here,* I thought to myself.

Roger continued. "I'm going to need a lot of help. Posters will be your job, Annie. I'll need a good speech for the rally. Dan, you can help me with that. And all of you—talk to your friends and your friends' friends. I think we can do it."

We talked about these jobs for a while. Then Roger told us about all the letters he was getting from colleges, for next year. Dan talked about where he might play football. I didn't have much to say. But they seemed to like my ideas for the posters. They were very nice to me.

After dinner, I was telling Mitch, ". . . and Roger's getting letters from all these colleges that want him to go there . . ."

75

"Like these?" Mitch asked, with a smile. He pulled a couple of letters off the table. They were for Mitch. "They send these to everyone, Annie."

"What do you know," I said. "And Roger made it sound like a big deal!"

I got to know Roger better as I worked with him. He was just a guy like Mitch—nothing special. Sometimes, he and Danny would sit around, talking about people. They'd say things like, "I'd never take her out. She has a nose like a ski jump." Or, "He plays as if he just got out of a wheelchair. He'll never make the team." They even talked that way about their own friends!

I told Mitch about that. "I'm not sure I want to help Roger anymore. I don't think he is the best one for the job."

"He doesn't sound like it," Mitch agreed. "But I don't think you should

Mitch pulled a couple of letters off the table.

quit. Everyone will think you're a quitter, and that you don't keep your word. You'll look bad, and he'll look good."

"I see what you mean," I agreed.

"Just wait, Annie. He can't pretend to be something he isn't. You caught on—so will other people. They'll see for themselves."

I wondered.

I made the posters as I said I would. But I hoped the other kids in school would find out what Roger was like before the election. Some people thought he was a great guy.

Just before the vote, there was a rally in the gym. Each candidate had to make a speech. Roger planned to make a speech with a lot of jokes.

"This job is a joke," he said. "So my speech will be a joke, too."

"Roger, I don't think that's a good

idea. Besides, why are you running if you think it's a joke?" I asked him.

"Annie, dear, just leave the thinking up to Big Roger," he said to me. Imagine, I used to think he was really something!

Most of the students came to hear the speeches. First, Rod Myers spoke. He is the guy who had been on the student council. His speech was about how he'd learned to work with teachers and students. He sounded so stuffy. Maybe Roger was right. We could use a joke.

Roger's speech had everyone laughing. When he was done, the whole gym cheered him. *Uh, oh,* I thought. *He fooled them like he fooled me. We'll have a year of "Big Roger" ahead of us for sure.*

Then Anita came out. She said, "You all know I've been a cheerleader. When I

"I think we can change this school, and make it better."

had that job, I stood for this school. There were things about this school I was proud of, and things I didn't like. I think we can change this school, and make it better..."

As she talked, everyone in the gym listened. They wanted to hear what she had to say. When she was done, she got bigger cheers than Roger.

The vote was close, but Anita won. I voted for her myself.

"What did I tell you?" asked Mitch later that evening. "After all, the best man...er, woman won. You know I'm always right."

"This time you *were* right, Mitch," I said. "For once." I try not to let him get too far out of line.

A Week on My Own

Each year, I go away to Lake Bluebird
with my family for spring break. And, it
is BORING! What can you expect from
a place called Lake Bluebird?

It's no secret that I don't like it. But I
never thought Mom and Dad cared how
I felt. Then, this year, Mom said,

"Mitch, Dad and I think you're old enough to make your own plans for your spring break."

I was stunned.

"What? I don't have to go along with you?" I asked.

"That's right," Dad added. "Just talk your plans over with us first."

"Yeah, sure." I didn't sound very excited. I was still in shock. I got used to the idea in a hurry, though. And my friends loved it.

"Are you lucky!" Craig said when I told him. "I'd give my right arm to be left home on my own. You can do anything you want."

"That's the hard part," I said. "I can't decide what I want to do."

"Stay out late. Throw a party. Make as much noise as you want," Craig said.

"Sure," I said, "so it'll never happen

*"Mitch, Dad and I think you're old enough to
make your own plans for spring break."*

again. Besides, every year I do the same things. I want to do something new. Maybe I'll go somewhere on my own."

"How about Las Vegas?" Louis suggested. "I'll go too."

"Sure, sure. Try to be helpful, guys." I was looking for some ideas. I wanted to do something special.

"I've got an idea," Ron said. "You cycle a lot — so take a bike trip."

"Hey, I like that," I said.

"I'll go too," said Louis, "even if it's not to Las Vegas."

We decided we'd all take a bike trip — Ron, Louis, Craig, and I. With them along, the trip would be even better, I thought.

I rode my bike every day to get in shape. I was really looking forward to this trip. It wouldn't be someone else's idea of a good time. If I planned it right,

Mitch rode his bike every day to get in shape.

it would be perfect.

At last, the day for the trip came. Mom and Dad told me about six times to be careful. Then Craig, Ron, and Louis rode around the corner. I said good-bye to Mom and Dad and rode off with my friends.

I was on my own, away from my family, at last.

My friends and I got as far as the hills outside town. Then we had a problem.

"Hey, guys! Slow down," Ron called.

I didn't feel like slowing down, but I did. I could still hear Ron panting.

"Can't you keep up?" I asked him.

"I'm going as fast as I can," he gasped.

I felt angry that he was slowing me down. "You said you'd be ready for this trip," I called back. "You said you didn't need to train."

"I thought I was in good shape," Ron

puffed. "Besides, I had a lot to do after school."

Yeah, I said to myself, *like eat pizza.* Well, I was going to ride the way I wanted. I started to speed up.

"Slow down, Flash," Craig called to me. "This isn't a race."

"Yeah," Louis added. "Take it easy."

"Do you mind?" I said. "I took this trip because I like to ride."

"So this is *your* trip now," said Craig. "Gee, I thought we were going to do something together."

"Yeah, it is my trip. You guys wanted to come with me. I'm not coasting the whole way."

"Well, coast or ride by yourself, then," Craig yelled back.

The road got steeper. No one said anything else. I was riding farther and farther ahead. If Ron couldn't keep up, why should I slow down? I wasn't going to change my plans for them. Maybe I should have gone alone.

I started to make good time. *Cool down*, I said to myself. *Don't let them spoil this.* I looked around. The road was edged by thick trees and tall weeds. I was alone in a deep valley of green. All I heard was the whir of my own bike wheels.

The sun was shining brightly—a perfect day. Then I noticed something shiny up ahead. A car! The driver didn't see me. He pulled right across the highway from a side road. I was too close, going too fast.

Everything happened at once.

"Hey, look out!" I yelled. I made a quick turn and went right off the road. I saw the road, the car, the trees, and then the sky. I was lying on some gravel—my bike over my legs.

The driver must have heard me yell. He stopped his car and got out. "Hey, kid, are you okay? I didn't even see you."

I crawled out from under my bike. I'd lost a little skin and my wrist hurt. I stood up. My legs felt fine. The bike looked okay. I picked it up, and rolled it a few feet.

"Yeah, I'm okay," I told him.

"Are you sure?" the driver asked again.

"Yeah, I'll be fine. The bike's okay, too."

He drove off slowly. I got back on my bike and started off.

Then I heard a sharp ping! Uh oh, I knew what that sound meant. This was not my day. I got off the bike and looked at the wheels. Two spokes were broken.

Mitch crawled out from under his bike.

It would have been easy enough to fix — if my wrist didn't hurt.

I sat down to fix the bike. It was going to be slow work.

That's when the others caught up with me.

"Hey Mitch! How's life in the fast lane?" Craig yelled when he first saw me. I felt pretty silly sitting there. "Hey, what happened to you?" He wasn't laughing after he saw the scrapes on my arms and legs.

"I fell off the bike. I'm okay, but my wrist hurts. And I broke a couple of spokes."

"Boy, are you slow!" Louis said. "Here, let me take care of those spokes."

"Yeah, now I'm slowing *you* down," I said. That was my way of saying I was sorry.

"You probably fell just to make us feel

better," Ron said. That was Ron's way of saying it was okay.

"But just slowing down would have been fine," Craig added. "You didn't actually have to get into an accident. You always get carried away."

We all laughed. Only my friends could make a day like this seem funny.

Well, this trip wasn't going to be perfect. But it was still going to be special, thanks to my friends.